Maxi's Bed Magicians

atomium books

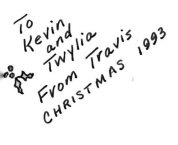

To
Kevin
and
Twylia
From Travis
CHRISTMAS 1993

Maxi's Bed Magicians

A picture-story by Werner Blaebst
English adaptation by Seán Bourke

atomium books

It was Monday morning.

Maxi lay awake in the early morning stillness.
He could hear his father snoring, but Maxi was waiting
for another sound.

Finally, it came . . .

"How I hate Monday mornings," Dad muttered, as he stumbled from his big bed to the bathroom.

Mom stretched and yawned. "I'll fix breakfast," she said sleepily, shuffling to the kitchen.

Maxi stomped into their bedroom with a big smile. He closed the door and said softly, "Hi, magicians."

For Maxi and the magicians, Monday morning
meant fun-time.

"Okay, guys, we're all alone," whispered Maxi.
"Are you ready?"

You don't have to ask bed magicians twice.
They just LOVE to play!

Climbing on the TV set, Maxi stretched out his arms
and called, "Here I come . . .

Ready . . .

Set . . .

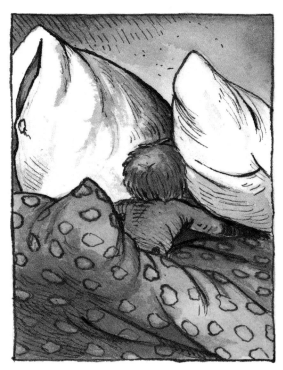

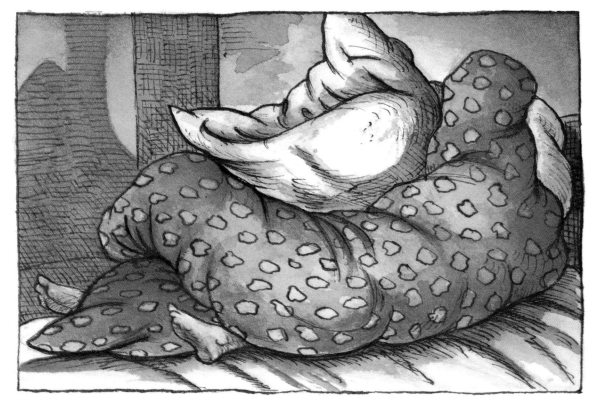

Maxi landed on the pillows with a PLUMPS! It was so lovely, soft, and warm snuggling there with his friends.

"This is even better than watching television," Maxi said to the magicians. "But I wish one day I could have an exciting adventure, just like on TV."

"I suppose you'd like to be the hero," asked his favorite bed magician with a grin.

"You bet!" said Maxi.

"Okay then, here goes," said the biggest magician. "If you can get through this adventure, we'll make you our king."

As the bed magician spoke, his voice got softer and softer and softer . . .

Maxi found himself all alone in a great big desert. The covers had turned into vast stretches of sand and the pillows had become distant hills.

"Where are you?" he called to the bed magicians. No one answered.

Maxi knew that he had to travel through this strange land to reach the end of his adventure. But it looked so big.

Maxi tried to climb a steep pillow-mountain.

"How will I get to the top?" he wondered. "Hey, magicians! On TV the hero always has a horse to help him climb hills, doesn't he?"

No one answered.

At the top of the mountain, a huge pillow came hurtling down
on top of Maxi.

Right before his eyes, the pillow twisted and turned into
a beautiful white horse. Maxi climbed on the horse and rode off
across the strange landscape.

After a long ride, Maxi came to a bed-sea.
How would he cross it?

On the beach Maxi spotted a piece of driftwood
in the shape of a button.

When Maxi bent to pick up the driftwood, his horse twisted
and turned into a pillow-raft. What an adventure!

As Maxi paddled across the water, he closed his eyes
and pretended to be a famous explorer on the high seas.

Oh, no! What was this?

Towering over Maxi was a giant
bed-wave. It was going to roll right
over him . . .

Maxi mounted his piece of driftwood like a surfboard and rode the giant wave.
"Wheeeeeeeeeeeeeeeeee. This is just like in Hawaiiiiiiii," sang Maxi.

But then, the wave rolled into a hole . . .

Down, down, down fell Maxi into the deep, dark bed-hole. He fell so fast it took his breath away. With a THUD he hit the bottom.

"Some landing," groaned Maxi, rubbing his sore backside.

There was no time to rest. Suddenly everything began swirling round and round and round. It was like riding on the top of a tornado.

"Hey, guys, give me a break!" moaned Maxi.

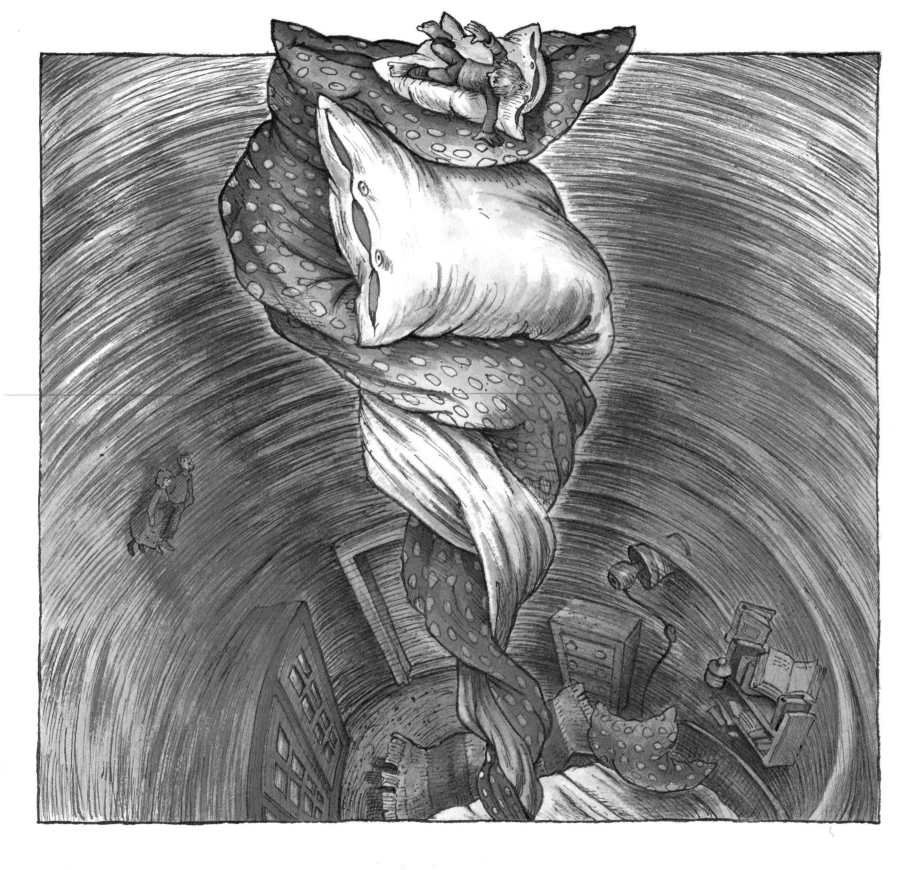

Then a voice boomed out, "Congratulations, Maxi! You've made it Now you can be our king."

Maxi opened his eyes and found himself sitting on a towering bed-throne — just made for heroes and kings.

"King Maxi," whispered a small bed magician. "Would you like to rest for a while?"

"Yes, but just for a minute," smiled Maxi And he followed the little magician into a secret cave. Maxi closed his eyes . . .

"MAXIIIIII! MAXIIIII!" It was Dad. "Come on, son. Breakfast is ready."

The bed magicians formed a guard of honor as King Maxi marched off.

On his way to the kitchen, Maxi could still hear the rolling waves . . .

First published in the United States 1990 by

Atomium Books Inc.
Suite 300
1013 Centre Road
Wilmington, DE 19805.

First edition published in German by K. Thienemanns Verlag, Stuttgart-Wien, 1986,
under the title "Maxis Bettmonster."
Text and pictures copyright © K. Thienemanns Verlag 1986.
English translation and adaptation copyright © Atomium Books 1991.

Printed and bound in Belgium by
Color Print Graphix, Antwerp.
First U.S. Edition
ISBN 1-56182-020-2
2 4 6 8 10 9 7 5 3 1